The Lodestone Files

The Cat, The Mouse, and The Thing from Another World

Among Us: Contact, Assimilation, Control, Extermination Series
Book Two

Robert J. S. T. McCartney

A.B.Normal Publishing and Media Group™

A.B.Normal Publishing and Media Group
PO Box 31311
Knoxville, TN 37930
www.abnormalpublishing.com

Publisher's note: This is a work of fiction. Names, characters, places, and incidents are a product of the author's imagination. Locales and public names are sometimes used for atmospheric purposes. Any resemblance to actual people, living or dead, or to businesses, companies, events, institutions, or locales is completely coincidental.

Book Layout © 2014 BookDesignTemplates.com

The Lodestone Files: The Cat, The Mouse, and The Thing from Another World / **Robert J. S. T. McCartney** — Second Print, 2020

To my wife, Karyn, and my kids, Zelda and Aeris.

To my friends and family.

"Be anything but normal."

—**Robert J. S. T. McCartney**

Be sure to look for these great titles and more.

The Chronicles of Bob: The Chronic Suicidal by Robert J. S. T. McCartney, available now.

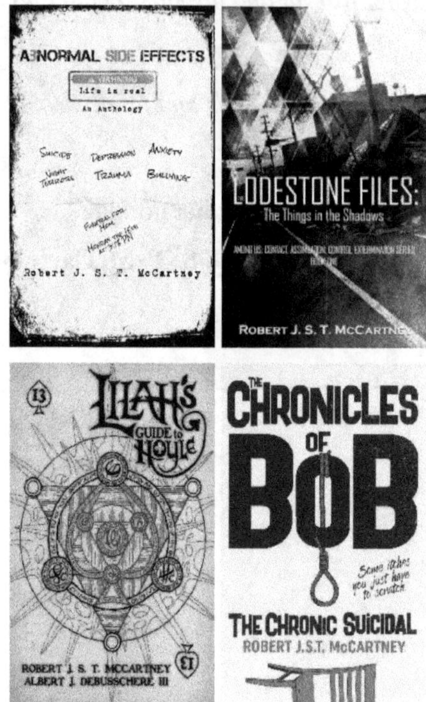

Visit www.abnormalpublishing.com for free stories, information, and more.

Contents

Chapter One

THE SUN SHINED brilliantly. Birds chirped, the grill sizzled, people played in the park. It was just another great day out. Idris smiled as he watched his dad and Cal flip burgers and turn the hot dogs, while his mom set out paper plates for the meal.

People passed by and complimented James and Cal on their cooking, saying that they were jealous and wished they could have some. Of course, being the good neighbor he was and being prepared, James had Idris give out some plates of cheeseburgers and chili dogs to others.

As they all sat down and enjoyed their meal, the bright day turned dark. A shadow loomed high that blacked out the sun. Red vines spiraled down from the heavens and began to snatch up people. Marionette-like figures came and assaulted people, assimilating them. Soon, there was little difference between friend and foe…or family.

Idris and his family had attempted to flee but only watched in horror the monsters ripped his mom apart. He had tried to call out to her, but nothing came out. Her limbs pulled every which way, while they fought over her insides like spilled bags of candy on Halloween. His father corralled them towards an alleyway. Together, they dodged the encroaching red vines and packs of aliens that took on their host's form: animals, kids, people; it didn't matter. As they made it into the alleyway, Idris caught sight of a little girl leaping up to a man and tearing out his throat with a hideous maw.

Fear. Anxiety. The looming specter of death that closed in behind them. James pointed towards the door to a building, and the boys ran to it. Idris crossed the threshold first and then heard the horrifying scream of his father. He turned around and saw his father being devoured by a dark red blob, slowly dissolving. Cal slammed the door shut, and the boys continued to run downstairs that seemed to go on forever.

Eventually, the stairs led them to an underground bunker. Here they met a strange man in a lab coat. The man held an unrecognizable weapon and pointed it at the boys.

"You, you're not human, you're one of *them*," the man shouted.

At first, he was aiming at Idris, but it then drifted to Cal. Darting in front of his brother and shielding him, he felt a strange sensation from his back. He looked down and saw red vines protruding through his stomach and slowly beginning to tear him open. Slowly he got spun around, where he saw his little brother grinning sadistically.

His lips moved, a disembodied voice spoke. “You trusted your family so much, and it led to your downfall. Thank you for leading me to the doctor. He was the only one that could have stopped all this.”

A man in a black suit and sunglasses emerged from behind the 'imposter' of his brother and executed. He knelt next to the dying Idris and offered him a mercy kill. The last moments Idris remembered before waking up was hearing the name "Murdoch."

***

He awoke to the sound of the truck door being slammed shut. Cal slept next to him, peacefully. Idris was impressed at how resilient his little brother was. The realization came back again, setting in once more; his parents were dead, the whole town wiped out. He and his brother were the only survivors, and they were being hunted down by an alien that could assimilate the people it absorbed.

Then there was the drunkard who had a shady past that saved them from death back in Lodestone.

Although, Mac claimed that he had known about the 'Thing's' presence and that there was a race of these monsters; that with a treaty in place, the aliens were able to feed on isolated populaces so they can reproduce, and in exchange, we received otherworldly resources. Even with clear evidence by some conspiracy theorists, they were all dismissed as tinfoil hat sightings and shenanigans. On top of that, the government made sure to 'silence' them all. Of course, the U.S. Government suggested it doesn't just let them feed whenever they want without repercussions.

Mac came out of the gas station. He slowly climbed into the truck and set off for anywhere but there.

"Can't sleep," he asked.

Idris shook his head, "No, I had a bad nightmare." He thought about where exactly they'd be going. "So, are we heading anywhere in particular?"

Mac sighed. "I can't say exactly, but I've gotten word from a contact that wants to blow this thing wide open. The only thing is, is they are on their schedule and well…" He ran his fingers through his hair, scratching his scalp.

"What?"

"He could be luring us because of his higher-ups, but I've known the guy, and it's not like him to get this desperate. He never contacts me."

"So, it's unusual behavior for him?"

Mac nodded as he started the truck up. "Very."

The truck then set off for its new destination, not realizing they were being followed.

Some miles down the road, Mac gave notice now and then at the vehicle that was distancing itself and making the same turns as them.

"I think we have a problem, kid."

"What's that," asked Idris.

"We're being tailed. It's probably a cleaner."

Idris looked in the mirror to try and get an eye on the vehicle that assumingly followed them. "A cleaner? What—who the hell is that?"

"An agent of the government that does one thing. Clean up messes or take people out." Mac rubbed his forehead with a sigh, "This is not my week."

Soon enough, they were back on the open road with trouble right on their heels.

Chapter Two

MURDOCH TURNED THE turned the volume up on the stereo as a dispatch agent came over. "Go to Hell," he grunted in disgust.

He readied his handgun, eager to put the fugitives down, and report to his superior.

Cars would buzz by, ruining his chance. Some were bold enough to cut him off.

He sighed and decided that all formalities and consideration had gone out the window. He had a job to do.

Murdoch pressed his foot on the accelerator, down to the floor. The car's engine roared with ferocity as it surged forward on the pavement. It tapped the back bumper of the vehicle that had just passed him.

From the driver window of the car in front of him, there emerged a middle finger and then a gun.

Murdoch grinned at the gesture. He let off the gas slightly, then rammed the car again, causing it to go off the road and crashing into a few boulders off the side of the way.

A few gunshots could be heard from behind him as he sped on after the water truck.

***

"Looks like he wants to play a game. Alright, kid, you're up," said Mac.

"What? You want me to kill him?" asked Idris.

"Kill or disable. I don't care what. I prefer the first, though," Mac said.

Idris took his father's gun and readied himself.

"Idris, what's going on?" Cal asked, yawning.

"Cal, I'm going to need you to feed ammo to me and stay quiet."

"What? Why? What's going on?"

"Listen to your brother, and stay low. We're going to deal with our little problem," said Mac as he looked in the mirror. "Get ready, kid. Here he comes!"

The car rammed the water truck from behind; it's occupants jerking forward. Mac maintained control and kept driving. "Go, go!" he ordered.

Idris leaned out the window slightly and fired a shot at the car's windshield, making a hole in it.

"Ha, it looks like the government cut funding on bulletproof glass for his ride," grinned Mac. "Keep it up, kid."

The car sped up again. Idris braced for impact and readied another shot. He fired at the radiator and then another few more shots at the windshield; the car swerved, then came up alongside them. The window came down, and Idris could see he had hit the assailant. Shots erupted from the driver's window, making holes in the back left tires. Idris fired out several more shots at the man. Soon, the car was but a speck in the distance.

***

"I'll give it to that kid; he's a good shot." Murdoch grunted as he tried to patch up his bleeding arm and shoulder.

Soon a familiar car had caught up to him. It stopped next to him, and an enraged male driver came around to have words with him.

Murdoch sighed at the man's fast approach and arsenal choice of words.

"You piece of shit, no good, mother fucker! I'm going to end you!"

"Excuse me, but you're in my way," said Murdoch as he shot the man in the leg.

"What the fuck is wrong with you," cried the man who laid in pain on the ground.

Murdoch crouched next to the man. "Well, I could have just killed you, I thought I was rather generous. Should I reconsider?"

The man waved his hands, "no, no, no, we're cool, man, we're cool."

Murdoch smiled, "Good. See you around…friend."

He then got in the man's car and sped after the fugitives.

***

“Since we’ve been made, we need to get a new ride,” said Mac as he struggled to maintain control of the municipal water truck.

Idris stared hard at the upcoming traffic sign. “The sign there says about five miles. Can we make it?”

Mac grunted, “Yeah, I—I think I can. Just keep an eye out for that guy.”

Idris glanced in the right mirror and saw nothing. At least, not yet.

Cal tugged at his arm. “Idris, I’m hungry.”

“Oh, I’m sorry, Cal,” Idris said as he took the knapsack and searched for something for Cal to eat. “Here.”

Cal took the granola bar package and opened it, hastily eating it.

“You feel alright, buddy?”

“I—I dunno. I still can’t feel my ankle. I can kind of move it, I just, I can’t explain it. I don’t feel like I am me.”

Idris felt his stomach turn, and the vision of his nightmare flashed for a second, causing him to hold his breath. Mac looked over at the boys and then back to the road.

"We're going to have to make this quick. If it is anything, you may be getting infected by the alien's spores. Those "vines," they secrete a toxin." Mac sighed. "Even though you might not see anything visible, it'll get in your skin, burrow, get in your blood, and replicate like crazy. Eventually, you're just a zombie—and I don't mean a brain muncher, but you're trapped in your body; inside looking out, lights on upstairs but no one's there."

The truck jerked violently and swerved off the road—another tire had gone. “Shit!” Mac slammed his fist on the steering wheel. “We need to get moving now!”

Whether by chance or fate, they happened to be near a house not too far from their location. “There,” Mac pointed, “get going. We’ll take whatever they have there.”

Mac and the boys all rushed out of the truck. Idris carried Cal via piggyback and rushed as fast as he could behind Mac.

The house was a quaint little bungalow, with plenty of rocks and more rocks littering the yard. There was an occasional cactus here or there but nothing substantial or green. The curtains in the windows were all drawn shut, suggesting that either no one was home, or no one wanted visitors. On the side entrance, however, there was a red pickup truck, and that just happened to be the ticket.

Mac immediately set to break into the truck and ordered Idris to keep watch. Idris thought he heard a noise coming from inside the house—a clamoring—or that one all too familiar sound.

I know that sound.

Mac hopped in the truck and searched for any keys. Idris put Cal in and got in himself.

“Yes!” Mac said as he flipped the sun visor down, and the truck’s keys fell into his hands.

Idris then heard that noise again nearby, and he remembered. “Shotgun!”

“The hell you people doin’ in my truck! Get the fuck out!” An older man held a shotgun in their direction and fired a shot that hit the side of the barn, not too far off from them.

“Shit, shit, shit!” Mac grunted as he stuck the keys in the ignition, and put the truck in gear and sped off.

"You sons of bitches!" The man shouted as he fired another series of shots at the fleeing vehicle, striking the right rear taillight.

"Are you OK," Idris asked Cal.

"I'm fine, just tired," he replied.

Mac rubbed his face and ran his fingers through his hair. "Alright, you two stay low. Idris, you keep that gun handy. Next chance we can, we're gonna stop at a motel, rest up, and hopefully play it off. I'll get in touch with my contact and see if he can meet us somewhere."

Both boys nodded.

***

Murdoch drove the car hard, so hard in fact that he had to let it sit a few times off the side of the road. Several people had stopped but fled once they saw he had been bleeding and his rough disposition.

Luckily, the one road rage driver hadn't called the police yet, so he supposed he was in good spirits. He turned the key and started the car up again. This time he had to catch up or at least get a new vehicle.

No more games. No more "by the book" nonsense.

Murdoch's superiors and other agents admired his cutthroat attitude but also his wit, where he'd go by the book to drive a knife through someone's back. For this reason, he rose fast in the agency and was a favorite by his newest...boss.

The car roared, and the dust billowed behind him. Soon enough, he came upon the water truck. He pulled over and got out, gun in hand. He investigated it and sighed. There were no clues for him to go on. Nothing. He planted a small batch of C4 on the water truck and car and detonated it.

Someone will be through here soon enough. Until then, I suppose it's time for a nature walk.

He looked over and saw a house not too far off from where he was. "Maybe I can get a spot of water."

Chapter Three

"AH, AS I was telling your compatriot here," James pointed to the dead soldier on the ground, "I am so pleased to meet you. I ask you, politely, from one human," he put his finger up in the air, "Ah dammit, I mean, man to man—"

"PUT YOUR FUCKING HANDS UP!" An armed soldier pointed his assault rifle at James.

James smirked. "Please, I am not your enemy. Your government is to blame."

"This is Bravo-13, I have "Chemical X" in custody. I need backup, ASAP, over!" The soldier radioed.

James sighed. "Do you think that your little *squad* is going to save you? I was blown to kingdom come!" He threw his arms up, "and guess what, boys? I'm still here." He laughed hysterically, "That is so cute!"

Soon, a group of armed soldiers came and surrounded him. "Now, now, boys. How do you think this is going to end, huh?" He paced around in a circle, with both arms out wide. "You know you're just throwing your lives away, and for what?"

"ON THE GROUND! NOW," the soldiers ordered.

"Alright then," James sighed, "you can't say I didn't give you a fair warning," he calmly said, cracking his neck.

Several vines protruded from James' back and impaled the soldiers' throats. "You know, it is getting rather bothersome working alone as of late. My brothers and sisters, well, they weren't the strongest in the evolution stew, but that's alright. When you want something done right, you've got to do it yourself."

The soldiers went from the lifeless husks to jittering, fast flinching. Their eyes glowed a fierce red. Slowly the vines returned to their home, and the soldiers now worked for him.

"Alright, maggots, it's time for you to spread the good word! I want the bastard responsible for blowing me up…and then I want those kids." He spat on the ground. "Dismissed!"

James could hear the radios going abuzz with chatter. He was done with hiding and abiding by terms set by a lesser race. It was war now, and he held no rules.

As the soldiers ran rampant through the town, eliminating other soldiers and further spreading his ability to control other bodies, James came to absorb the knowledge and information of those higher up.

"It seems I am taking a road trip," he grinned. "Don't worry, boys; daddy is coming for you."

***

The man removed his glasses and wiped his brow. He was sweating profusely, and the server room wasn't helping his disposition at all. He changed some cable connections around and inserted a flash drive into one of the ports.

"I pray that this gets out and the people revolt. I hope I am not too late," he said softly.

"Hey, what are you doing back there?" A security guard shined his flashlight at the suspicious man near the server towers.

"Just some maintenance. There are some loose connectors and tangled—" the man started to say.

"I don't give a fuck if you were the Pope. There's no scheduled maintenance today, and you sure as hell ain't anyone I've seen down here before," the security guard said.

The man put his glasses back on. "Well, then I suggest you run, run as fast as you can."

The guard drew his gun, "Step away from the servers, NOW!"

"I can't do that, sir."

"STEP AWAY! NOW!"

"I am sorry for this." The man then sighed a final time. There was a click and then a bright flash that engulfed the room. What followed was a series of explosions throughout the building. It eventually had all collapsed onto itself and was laid to rest as a smoldering heap.

The Internet received the message; all news and media outlets, emails, everywhere. It was the call for people to wake up.

Chapter Four

IN A DARK motel room, the two brothers slept.

Mac sat at the table by the door, gun in hand. He felt his chest pocket vibrate, and out of habit reached for his phone. Mac saw it was a text message from his contact.

The message has been sent. The world knows. I am sorry, friend. They will say things about me on the news most likely but don't believe it. Find Albrecht at the bunker. He might be able to help your companion's brother. Tina will be all right on her own. — Jack

Mac sighed as he tossed the phone on the table, "Ah, dammit, Jack."

Idris woke up, startled by the noise. He looked over to see Mac with his head in his hands. "Everything alright, Mac?"

"Yeah, sorry, kid. Just got some bad news is all."

"I'm sorry to hear that," said Idris as he got out of bed.

Idris yawned and sat down in the chair across from Mac. He grabbed a package of jerky and soda can and began to eat and drink.

"My contact," Mac started, "he was my brother, Jack. He was a scientist: a true egghead like no other. Jack also was in some of the government's deepest shit. He used to be loyal, followed the book, everything. Then, when some experiment went wrong at a lab that opened a portal to another world, …things changed. The first expedition team went AWOL. Then the next team went, which he was a part of. He saw these things, these dark, sinister beings that acted like puppets and their hosts' bodies like puppets. Shapeshifting, parasitic, red vines, and an insatiable appetite. He watched them feed on the Alpha team, and some Alpha team members feed on the Bravo team." Mac looked down at the phone.

“He ran. He ran as fast as he could back to the portal. Then he got cornered.” Mac sighed. “He was brought before their alpha. There they proposed something ideal for both parties. That they access the portal to Earth and breeding grounds, food, in exchange for resources native to their planet. Of course, he said yes, but he would have to bring a proper representative before the alpha.” Mac poured a shot of whiskey and drank it, then poured another one.

“Then the world’s head leaders all came to know that “life exists in the universe.” Boy, were they stupid to think that we were ever alone. Eventually, the treaty was drafted, signed, and the two sides went to working with one another immediately. Small towns or unmarked habited places were first. They’d bring in a cleanup crew to replicate the city, restore any damage, and synthesized humans or actors. No one would ever be the wiser."

Mac took another shot of whiskey. "Jack felt horrible for unleashing those aliens onto the world. All the resources we had gained were used for military purposes and treating diseases that only the one percent could ever hope to afford and the top politicians. Then they began plans for if the aliens attacked us. They figured out they worked like a hive when they followed some at a feeding. They found out how they bred; they evolved, everything. There were some repercussions at first, but the world leaders worked it out when they offered a bigger slice of the pie at the feeding. The result also unleashed an outbreak which the government disguised as Ebola. Of course, it was dismissed of anything being serious, let alone that it was them being responsible. That people were going missing, being eaten for breeding purposes, or even becoming assimilated. Soon, the aliens had begun to take on new forms, infiltrate the government ranks; it was a grand scheme of spy vs. spy. However, Earth could close the portal whenever it wanted."

"They never closed it," Idris asked.

Mac shook his head. "Nope, they kept it open, for a while anyway. There was some talk that it had been closed, but I can't say. I'd have to get Jack's notes." He sighed. "Also, he said there's a guy that can help with your brother, but, we'd have to get to what we called 'the bunker.'"

"What's that?"

"It's a secret place we made with some of the other folks that didn't believe in the 'great good' of the relationship between them and us," Mac exaggerated with his hands. "In the event, we can't help him, kid, you gotta assume the worst. You'll have to prepare yourself if you need to stop him."

"That's not going to happen," Idris said sternly.

"Look, I get it, he's your brother; he's family, and you're willing to do whatever it takes. Hell, even if that means you are making a deal with a demon or Death." Mac's tone turned serious, "but you have to be ready for everything. We all go sooner or later," said Mac.

"If I have to cut that foot off of his, I will, but I am not losing my brother to some alien," Idris said frustratingly.

"Alright, I ain't gonna argue with you, but just so you're aware. If you don't do it, someone else will out there," said Mac.

"Are you implying that you would," Idris asked.

"Yes, without hesitation," Mac replied.

Idris clenched his fists, but reason and rationality sank in. "Alright."

Outside there was a car that could be heard that came to a screeching halt. A car door that opened and never closed.

Mac looked out the window and saw the man that attacked them earlier, looking at each motel window. "Shit, we've got company. We need to get out of here now! Get your brother and everything."

The trio snuck out the bathroom window and slinked across the street to the restaurant. Mac would nonchalantly check over his shoulder but found that they were not being followed. They took a booth seat inside and waited to see if the man would be thrown off their trail.

Shortly after that, the man had given up, so it seemed, and they all breathed a sigh of relief. To celebrate their "victory," they had each ordered a meal. Cal, however, ordered far much more than he was used to consuming.

Idris looked at his brother. "Cal, are you sure you can eat all that?"

"Yeah, I am starving," he replied.

Mac looked to Idris and gave him a nod.

Idris clenched his fists under the table, recalling Mac's warning and the nightmare he had earlier.

I won't let anything happen to you, Cal. I swear on it.

***

"Status report, Mr. Murdoch."

He growled at the voice, "I am on their trail, sir."

"Good. However, it seems we have another problem. Well, two more issues to contend with." The man on the end of the line sighed.

"Sir?"

"It seems the bioengineer and scientist that brought us in contact with the aliens has leaked information to the public."

Murdoch ran a hand over his face. "Do I need to take him out?"

"No, the poor bastard killed himself and blew up the research facility in New York, along with everyone in it. We've already released a cover-up story that I am sure the people will eat up endlessly," the man said.

"OK, so, what's the problem then?"

"The Lodestone incident…is not contained. The alien has killed the cleanup crew and infected several squads. It is initiating a war against us and is starting to pick off head members one by one. No one on their side wants to help, naturally, and claims that it is working on its accord. In short, we're about to face mass genocide if that thing succeeds in feeding and assimilating all in its path, let alone a full-scale invasion from the other side."

"Portal status?" Murdoch asked.

"It's down, which has upset the aliens a great deal. However, we're reaching a deal with them until this situation is resolved." The man sighed, "politics—in space, and otherwise, nothing is ever satisfied."

"What is needed from me then, sir?" Murdoch kept inspecting vehicles and glancing at motel windows to see if anyone was watching.

"I need you to eliminate that walking garbage disposal, TS-21, permanently. Then, you can pursue the kids and that rogue agent. You have 24 hours, Mr. Murdoch."

Murdoch sighed, "Yes, sir."

He had found the truck at last. The plate, make, and model all matched. He glanced inside of it and found nothing of usefulness.

They're close.

Murdoch put a tracking beacon underneath the truck and wandered back to the front office of the motel.

***

"Today, there was a terrorist attack against the sovereignty of the United States of America, an attack that took the lives of many American citizens. A terrorist acting alone with no known ties to any other groups leaked falsified information to allegedly lay blame on the government, that we were selling out our citizens and our allies. That is simply not true. We take the privacy and lives of our citizens and our allied forces seriously. We would never jeopardize the safety and integrity of them, let alone trade services with aggressive needs.

This man took the lives of several hundred men and women, some of the most bright minds in our days; the lives of exceptional people who would be working to provide a better future, cures, and more. This man perpetrated us as working with "aliens" and that they were among us, feeding on us, and other hysterical claims. These are nothing short of fiction and the rantings of a madman. My fellow Americans, I pledge to you that we are instilling the safety to screen those within would do us harm and threaten our future. I urge you to disregard this madman's ravings, and that we all stand united. I encourage you to trust in your government—your state and local leaders. We want to instill and ensure that we are the best country in the world, and that you are in safe hands.

Thank you."

The president stepped away from the podium, whereas then another man stepped up and commented something incomprehensible over the uproar of the reporters and people demanding answers.

Mac shook his head. “You weren’t kidding when you said they would demonize you.” He looked down at the laptop screen. He had begun going through the files his brother had sent before his death. Plans of invading the aliens’ world, counter-attack plans, diagraphs of their anatomy, chemical composition, and more. It was more than he needed, and a hell of a lot more than what he wanted.

Idris looked over at Mac while he picked at the remnants of his food. "What's all that?"

"A whole lot of shit. Stuff that will make your head spin, and is surely making the government's head spin. I wouldn't be surprised if the aliens catch hold of this and decide to invade. If they do, well, we're fucked solid."

Idris' stomach turned, causing him to push his plate away. Cal looked over at it and proceeded to clean the plate.

"Must be having a growth spurt there, Cal," Idris smiled, trying to make light of the situation.

Cal just sat there with a blank stare on his face, the comment going over his head. "Huh? Oh, sorry, I spaced out for a second there."

Idris looked to Mac. "You're gonna have to come to a decision, kid, and I prefer it sooner than later."

Idris gritted his teeth. "I am thinking about it. What about that doctor of yours you mentioned your brother said could help?"

Mac nodded, "It's a drive, so I suggest you take a piss or shit now."

Idris looked to Cal, "Hey, do you need to go to the bathroom? Now is a good time."

Cal shook his head, "No, I am fine."

Idris nodded and silently left the table for the restroom. *Please, God, don't take my brother from me.*

***

The door opened, revealing a distressed older man.

James flashed a grin. “Hello, sir, I am looking for a man and two boys. They may have been through here. Have you seen them?”

“You’re the second guy that’s come ‘round today askin’ for those, little shits,” said the old man.

“I see. Troubles with them?”

“Bastards stole my truck! They’re lucky I’m not a good shot anymore,” the man replied.

“Hmm, you mentioned that another person was looking for them?” James surveyed the area to see if there was anyone else around.

“Yeah, some agent—F.B.I. or something. He looked pretty beat up.”

“Quick question, do you live alone?” James cracked his knuckles.

“Huh? Oh, uh, yeah. Mavis, my wife, bless her soul—"

James rolled his eyes, “That’s enough.”

A red vine erupted from James' backside and penetrated the older man's neck. "Let me see…" Images, memories, and more flashed before James' eyes. "Hmm, she was quite the looker, my friend. My condolences." Then there were the images of Mac and the boys, then a picture of Murdoch. "Ah, it's Mr. Murdoch. I knew he would become such a good agent," James mocked. Then there were some other images and sounds, and soon they became distorted. "What? What's happening?" James looked at him. "STOP RESISTING!" James backhanded him across the living room. "You humans and your whole "free will" nonsense. I admire your tenacity, but learn to give it up." James readjusted his person then spun on his heels.

“Stay right where you are! Don’t move!” A state trooper held James at gunpoint.

James stopped in his tracks and sighed slowly, annoyed. “Oh, come on! I have places to be! People to assimilate, a war to carry out!”

“You’re not going anywhere, you freak!”

James smirked and kept walking towards the trooper. “Go ahead, shoot me. I am sure it’ll be fantastic when it gets posted online. I have no problem “faking it” like some people do.”

“Sir—thing—whatever the hell you are, stay back!”

James chuckled. “What is it that young humans say nowadays? Ah, yes.” He waved his hands around and mocked the trooper, “Come at me, bro!”

The trooper emptied his clip into James. He approached the fallen suspect with caution and then got a surprise of his life.

“I told you I was good at faking it. Now, then, I am going to need your clothes, your boots, and your motorcycle.”

“What the hell are you,” asked the panicked trooper.

“Let’s not worry about that,” said James smugly as a vine pierced the trooper’s neck.

In a moment, he was outfitted in the trooper’s full uniform. He walked over to the motorcycle that was parked.

"You know, it is a beautiful day for a bike ride," said James as he started the bike's engine. "Don't worry, boys, daddy is coming home," he grinned as he put on the sunglasses.

[To be continued...]

Acknowledgments

Thanks to my wife for enduring my antics. You make me moist.

Thanks to the Vapors of Morphine, Buckethead, and countless others for fueling me with countless hours of great music on this project and others.

Thanks to my friends and family for your continued support.

John Carpenter for his adaptation of *Who Goes There?* as the 1982 classic *The Thing*.

John W. Campbell for penning *Who Goes There?* and paving the way for a fantastic franchise.

Those involved with *The Thing from Another World* and *The Thing [2011]*.

My *World of Warcraft* friends on the US server Aegwynn, and in the Horde guild, Revolt. You're all demoted to "Mushroom Stamped."

With love,

Sin

Anyone else I may have forgotten to mention...thank you.

About the Author

Robert J. S. T. McCartney loves to read and write about the strange and bizarre. He currently lives in Knoxville, Tennessee with his wife and kids.

His works include:

- *The Lodestone Files: The Things in the Shadows [Book One]*
- *Abnormal Side Effects*, an anthology.
- *Lilah's Guide to Hoyle*, with Albert J. Debusschere III. Demons, witches, and a dash of mayhem. Lilah gambles her life and the lives of others in this exciting urban fantasy novel.
- The Chronicles of Bob: The Chronic Suicidal, an urban fantasy novella, that explores what happens when Bob cannot die via suicide and the consequences that follow.

www.ingramcontent.com/pod-product-compliance
Lightning Source LLC
LaVergne TN
LVHW010842120826
845149LV00020B/3488
* 9 7 8 0 9 9 8 3 9 3 0 5 6 *